Witch Tales

Manjiri Limaye

RUPA
PUBLICATIONS INDIA

First published in 2012 by
Rupa Publications India Pvt. Ltd.
7/16, Ansari Road, Daryaganj,
New Delhi 110 002

Sales Centres:

Allahabad Bengaluru Chennai
Hyderabad Jaipur Kathmandu
Kolkata Mumbai

10 9 8 7 6 5 4 3 2 1

Illustrations by Friederike Kipkeew

Printed in India by
Gopsons Papers Ltd.
A-14 Sector 60
Noida 201 301

Contents

Introduction

Lia, the Ladybird

Dear Readers,

The title of this book must have surprised you. One keeps hearing about fairy tales. In fact, almost all children, be it anywhere in the world, grow up listening to these tales. But no one has probably ever heard of *Witch Tales*. And there is a good reason for that. The witches have never given much thought to sharing their stories. There were always enough little witches and wizards to listen to and enjoy these stories, so the witches never took their stories out of Witchland. Even I found them only by sheer coincidence. And I'll tell you all about that. But before that, let me tell you a little about myself.

I am Lia, a ladybird. I live in a beautiful forest in the heart of Fairyland, where I have a very interesting job. I work for Rosie, the fairy, who runs a shop that rents jewellery to fairies. But not the kind of jewellery you would imagine – no diamond earrings or gold rings or silver brooches. The fairies don't like that kind of stuff. They mostly like flowers. They love to wear jasmines in their hair or a chain of daisies around their neck or a rose pinned to their dress as a brooch. But unfortunately, they cannot wear any flower as an earring as their ears aren't pierced. And that is a shame because earrings would have looked really beautiful on their pretty little ears. So Rosie, clever fairy that she is, came up with a fantastic idea. She asked us little ladybirds and bugs and beetles to become earrings for the fairies when they had to go out for a party or picnic. All we had to do was sit pretty on the fairy's ears till the party was over. The fairies liked the idea very much and soon realised the advantages of such an earring. First, they found someone to match the dress they were wearing – a ladybird for a red frock, a shiny green beetle for a sparkling green dress, and so on. And having a bug on your ear makes sure that you don't miss out on anything because even when you are looking straight ahead, the bugs on your ears look to your left and right and softly whisper into your ear what is happening in the far corners of a room. And if you tell the bug beforehand at what time you intend to leave the party, you can just forget about it and enjoy the party. The bug will keep a watch on the clock and tell you when it is time to leave.

I love my job because, thanks to it, I get to attend so many parties I otherwise wouldn't have seen even from a distance. Once Fanny, the fairy, wanted to wear me as an earring to a party. It was the birthday of Gobby, the goblin and he was going to throw a lavish party in Goboland. He had invited all the goblins, fairies, pixies, witches, brownies and elves. Fanny was going to wear a red frock with black polka dots on it. A ladybird would go perfectly with it! Hence she chose me and my sister to be her earrings. I was as excited about the party as anyone who'd actually been invited, for I had never been outside Fairyland. And now I was to see a whole new land! But unfortunately, I hardly got to see anything. Fanny kept me and my sister in a box till we reached Gobby's garden. She was afraid that we would fall down while she was flying. So she wore us only when we were in Gobby's garden, which was beautiful but was like any other garden I had seen in Fairyland. So I was a little disappointed. But I soon forgot about that and started enjoying the party. But not Fanny. Poor Fanny had caught a cold while flying to Goboland. And her nose was running now and she kept sneezing. My sister and I were scared by this because, when she sneezed, her whole body, including her ears, shook so badly that we were afraid of falling off. So every time she sneezed, we held on to her ear tightly with all six legs and prayed that we wouldn't fall. But then came this big, huge sneeze – I just couldn't manage to hold on and flew straight into the pocket of the long, black cloak that the witch in front of Fanny was wearing. But nobody seemed to have noticed anything. Fanny started blowing her nose into her handkerchief and the witch went to join her friends for a dance. I tried to climb out of the pocket, but the witch kept dancing and I kept slipping back to the bottom of the pocket. I got exhausted after a few tries, so I just sat in the pocket, thinking of another way to get out. But I must have fallen asleep after that, for I never got to know when the party ended. I didn't hear the witch bidding goodbye to the other guests, nor did I feel anything when she climbed on to her broomstick and flew back to her home in Witchland.

I awoke the next day when the sun had risen already and the birds were chirping merrily. The cloak in the pocket of which I rested now hung on a nail in the witch's house. Through a small hole in the pocket, I saw the witch. She was now stirring something in a big, black cauldron. She didn't seem to have noticed anything. But her black cat had! He was staring at the black cloak with his big, round, green eyes – he could smell something. So he started mewing and pawing the cloak. At first, the witch didn't pay any attention to the cat, but when this strange behaviour did not stop, she got up and came to him. She took down the cloak from the nail and shook it hard, holding it upside down. And naturally, I fell out! The cat was about to pounce on me, but the witch picked me up just in time, placed me on one of her long fingernails and brought me up to the level of her eye. 'Hey there,' she said softly. But I had my eyes tightly shut as I was scared to death. She was a witch after all! The witch must have noticed that I was shivering, for she asked me, 'Hey, little ladybird, why are you so scared?' 'I ...

I ... I am scared of witches.' I blurted out. 'Why?', the witch asked. 'Because they are all evil, always mixing some evil potion in their cauldrons and casting cruel spells on others.' The words tumbled out before I could stop myself. 'Says who?' The witch's eyes widened in surprise. 'It's there ... it's there in some fairy tales!' I said triumphantly. If she was going to kill me anyway, let her at least know that everyone knew exactly what witches were like. I thought I would be thrown into the cauldron and boiled alive now. Imagine my surprise when the witch burst out laughing!

She shook so much while laughing that she had to set me down on a table so that I wouldn't fall down. The cat too looked at her quizzically. 'That's not true, little ladybird,' the witch said, wiping away the tears that had come to her eyes because of laughing so hard. 'I mean, yes, some witches are like that. But not all of them. And we do so many things other than making potions and casting spells. We go to school, do our housework, learn new things and do so much more. You would have known that if you had also read our *Witch Tales*.

'That sounds interesting,' I said, completely forgetting the fear I had felt earlier. 'Tell me a witch tale!' I cried, always eager to listen to a story. 'Why, I'll tell you many!'. laughed the witch.

'But you must have something to eat first. You have missed your breakfast. And hey, we haven't even introduced ourselves! I am Zischka. What is your name?' 'I am Lia,' I said, shaking one of her long fingernails with one of my tiny little feet. Zischka then gave me some deliciously fresh, green lettuce leaves. And as I munched on the leaves, she told me some of the most wonderful stories I've ever heard. Even as I was listening, I felt that I should take these tales to everyone who lived outside Witchland. And Zischka happily gave me permission to do so.

So here I am with some previously unheard but delightful stories just for you. It is my pleasure to present *Witch Tales* to you. And I hope you enjoy them as much as I did. Happy reading!

P.S.: Zischka's pet black cat Mischka was listening to the *Witch Tales* along with me. When he heard that I wanted to publish these tales, he also told me a story that he thought I should take out of Witchland. It is the story of why witches have pet cats and not pet dogs. So you will find Mischka's story inside this book as well.

Zora and the Moon

ONCE upon a time, there lived in Witchland a clever little witch named Zora. She had been one of the brightest students at the Witch School. She had learnt everything that makes a good witch – from flying on a broomstick to making potions in a big, black cauldron and choosing the right pet black cat. Zora had picked up everything so fast that she would often get bored in the classroom, waiting for the other witches and wizards to catch up. Seeing this, the old wizard, who was the principal of the school, encouraged her to take up extra-curricular activities. He personally taught her many other useful things like reading, writing and swimming.

As school drew towards an end, Zora, like most young people in this world, couldn't decide what she would do next. When asked what she wanted, she always gave the same answer. She used to say, 'Right now, all I want to do is to travel. I love to fly my broomstick and I fly it really well. But I am tired of flying it over the school ground. I want to take it high up and far away and see the big wide world.' Her parents, who were not the ones to force anything upon their child and who understood Zora's need and desire to explore the world, gave this plan their consent and Zora's joy knew no bounds.

Thus Zora set off. With each passing day, she flew higher and faster and further. She flew to the most exotic lands and met the most amazing creatures that exist on this earth. And whenever she came across a lake, river or sea, she parked her broomstick nearby, swam to the middle of the water and dived in deep. And there she met more amazing creatures. And everyone whom she met – be it the unicorn, kangaroo, mermaid or jelly fish – had a fascinating story to tell. Zora used to sit spellbound, listening to these stories. And when they had finished, all she could think of was how she could share these marvellous tales with the other witches and wizards in Witchland. And that was when she knew what she wanted to be. She wanted to be a writer and write about her travels – the places she had been to, the creatures she had met and the stories she had heard. Yes, that was it! So she flew back to her hometown, went straight to her father and borrowed from him a sheaf of plain white paper, a bottle of ink and a quill. 'I'll travel during the day, sleep a little in the evening and sit up writing at night,' decided Zora.

But there was a little problem. Zora's parents were very poor. They couldn't afford to buy her a bunch of candles or hire fireflies who would hover over Zora's desk all night, throwing light on it, helping her write. Zora thought of using a spell and creating some light for herself. But that would have disturbed her parents' sleep as they all slept in one tiny room, which was their home. So Zora decided to sit outdoors and write. Because, as her mother said, there can be no better writing lamp than the full moon that shines brightly every night.

Zora began her work that very night. She went to a grassy meadow far away from her home, close to the border of the town, where there would be nobody to disturb her. She spread a nice, warm, red rug on the grass and sat down on it with her papers. Zora was so excited about this new project that she stayed up writing the entire night. The next few nights too were really busy ones. But then, slowly, Zora started getting tired. The travelling and staying awake all night was wearing her out. After a few hours of writing, she would often fall asleep over her papers. The number of hours that she wrote became fewer with each passing night. And then, finally, after about fifteen days, came a night when she was so exhausted that she couldn't even write a single word. She slept the entire night. That one night's sleep really did her good; for the next morning, when she woke up, she was as fresh as the dew drops that twinkled on the leaves. So she started work again with much gusto. She worked a little more with each passing night, until a night came when she sat up writing the entire time. And then she again had to start cutting down on her writing hours.

This soon became a pattern with Zora. She would start work with tons of energy. She would travel the entire day and write the entire night. But slowly her body would start demanding rest. So she would cut down her working hours and then finally, at the end of a fortnight, take the whole night off. And then she would slowly increase her work all over again.

During the first few months, Zora used to be so engrossed in her writing and then so tired, and hence fast asleep, that she would hardly notice anything around her – neither the hooting of the owl, nor the insects that chirped and chatted away with each other through the night. But these little things soon started disturbing Zora. She would be unaware of them while writing, but after she had packed away her papers and quill and was trying to sleep on her red rug, they would begin to bother her. The hooting and the chirping were bad enough, but the worst thing was the bright moon that shone throughout the night. It really spoilt her sleep. Zora felt a little guilty blaming the moon like this. It was, after all, only because of him that she could write at night. 'I am really grateful to you,' Zora said softly one night as she lay on her rug, looking up at the moon. 'I just wish I could switch you off whenever I wanted to.' She smiled to herself at this absurd thought. But then she suddenly sat up straight. I know I can't switch it off, she said to herself, but maybe, maybe I can dim it as and when I please! 'Yes!' Zora jumped up excitedly at this thought. 'This

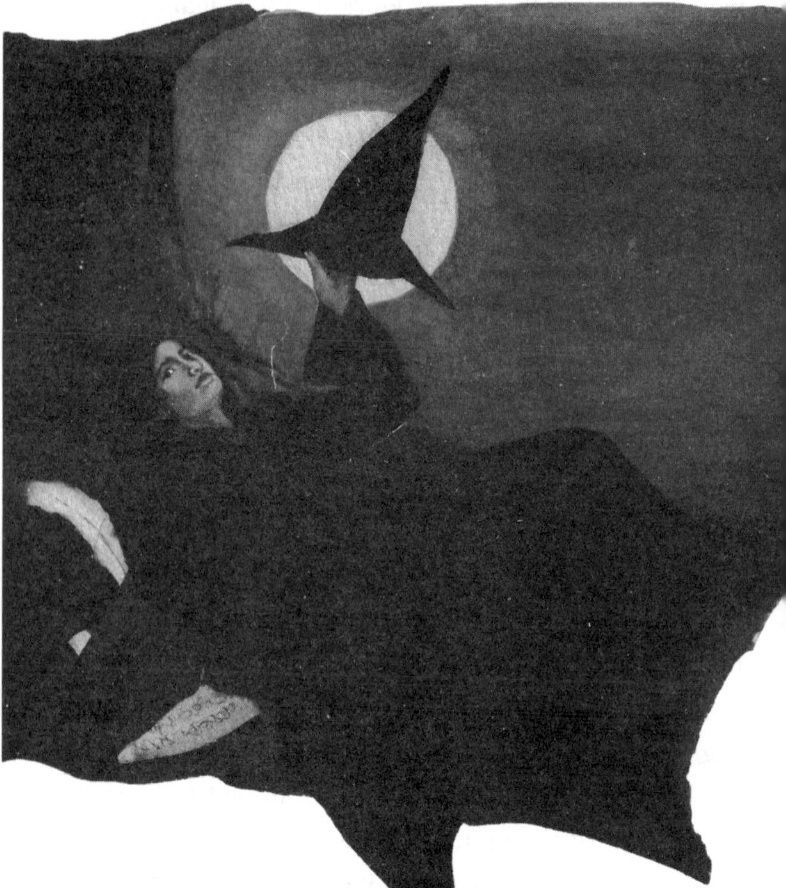

is the solution to my problem. Now all I need is to make the perfect potion and cast the spell!'

The next day, Zora was the first one to step into the town library after it opened. *Every Spell a Witch Would Ever Want to Know* read the title of the first book that she took down from a high shelf. 'Oh wizard! Am I a lucky witch!' She chuckled and quickly flipped open the thick, dusty book and scanned the index for 'Moon spells'. But there was nothing of the sort in there. So she got down on the floor and started reading the foreword. 'The science of spells has developed enormously, but, till now, there has been no spell known to witchkind that can affect the sun, moon or the stars,' stated the book. Bitterly disappointed, Zora slammed it shut.

She was extremely restless that night. It was the time when she was supposed to sleep all night, but the moon shone down mercilessly on her. Zora took her black, pointed hat and covered her face with it. But the moon still shone through. 'I should cover your face with this hat instead!' She glared at the moon. 'That's it!' cried Zora, as if struck by lightning, and jumped to her feet. 'I have found the solution! I should just cover up the moon! It is so simple – and here I was, rummaging through old books for spells!' Zora held up her hat against the moon. The hat was the right size but not the right shape for the moon. It was tall and pointy, whereas the moon was round and fat. Zora stared at the moon for a while and then decided that her big, black cauldron, which was also round and fat, should do the trick. Zora rushed to her house, fetched her cauldron, slung its handle onto the tail of her broomstick and took off. But poor Zora was to be bitterly disappointed once again. As she flew closer and closer to the moon, she saw it getting bigger and bigger. She hadn't even reached it yet and it already seemed a thousand times bigger than her cauldron. Dejected, she flew back to earth. 'Don't grin at me like that, you moon,' Zora said, shaking her little fist at it. 'I won't give up, I'll keep trying.'

The next day she went to the factory where her friends, the silkworms, worked. She asked them to use their silky strands to spin the moon into a cocoon. But as there were many weddings coming up in town, the silkworms were already working overtime to provide silk for the bridal trousseaus. They were extremely sorry, but they really had no time and couldn't help their friend. An unhappy Zora returned home.

Her mother, who was doing the housework when Zora came in, asked her what the matter was. 'Nothing Ma, I'm just having a really bad day,' replied Zora, who didn't want her mother to worry too much. 'Come here, my little Zoru.' Zora's mother pulled her close and tousled her hair. 'Do you want to help me a little with the housework? That should keep your mind off other things.' 'Okay,' said Zora. 'What do you want me to do?' 'Can you polish the copper plates that your aunt gifted us last year?' her mother asked. 'They have become really dirty and dull. Polish them till they become nice and shiny and bright.' 'I hate anything that is nice and shiny and bright!' yelled Zora and stormed out of the house, leaving a very puzzled mother behind.

Zora sat fuming in the grassy meadow. Then, suddenly, an idea struck her. She remembered what her mother had said, that the plates had to be polished because they were dirty and dull. So dirty was the opposite of clean and bright. 'Then I shall make the moon dirty!' Zora grinned mischievously. She fetched her cauldron again and filled it with all the soil and rocks that she could find. That night, she sat on her broomstick with the cauldron and flew once more towards the moon.

When Zora landed on the moon and looked around, she couldn't believe her eyes. The moon was nothing like she had imagined it to be. She had thought that it would be smooth and glossy and spotlessly clean. But now, as she looked at it, she saw that it was already covered with powdery soil and scattered rocks. There were even big holes in the ground. 'I don't understand this,' Zora said dolefully, still not believing what she was seeing. She sat down on the moon's surface and started weeping. She had run out of ideas to dim the moonlight.

'Hey, don't cry, little one,' said a voice out of nowhere. Zora almost jumped out of her skin. She looked around, trying to find the owner of the voice. 'Who ... who ... who is that and where are you?' she asked. 'I am the moon,' said the voice softly. 'Oh!' said Zora. 'I didn't know you could talk.' 'Of course I can talk!' the voice said indignantly. But then it softened again. 'What's the matter, little one?' asked the moon. 'Why are you crying? Can I do anything to help you?' 'Oh yes, you can!' Zora said eagerly, wiping away her tears. 'Could you please shine a little less each night? And then not shine at all for one night? And then start shining more and more again till you become your normal self?' Zora stopped to catch her breath and wondered if she had asked for too much. After a moment's silence, the moon said 'I am sorry, but I cannot help you, little one. You see, I can't help how much I shine. The moonshine you see is actually not mine. It is the sunlight. I reflect the sun's light and that's why people think that I shine.'

'Oh! I ... I didn't know that,' mumbled Zora and then stopped because she didn't know what to say. There was a moment's silence again. Then the moon spoke once more. 'But, little one, I am very curious. Why did you want me to shine differently every night?' 'That would have fit my writing schedule, you know,' Zora answered. 'You write?' exclaimed the moon. 'What do you write about?' 'I write about my travels,' said Zora. As she said this, she smiled in spite of herself, forgetting her worries.

Zora's face lit up as she started narrating her adventurous stories to the moon. Such was the charm that travelling held for her. Then she paused suddenly as a thought struck her. 'Can I ask you something, Mr Moon?' she asked a bit shyly. 'Don't you ever get bored? Being in the same place all the time, I mean? You should travel too!' Zora's eyes twinkled. 'Yes, you should travel. I can't tell you how fantastic it is! You can see so many different things and meet such amazing creatures. There must be so much to see in the sky. I saw so many stars and comets on my way to you. Travelling is fun. I could go on and on talking about it.' She stopped, thinking that maybe she was boring the moon. 'I think I should get going now. But it was nice meeting you, Mr Moon!' And with that, she jumped up on her broom and flew off.

The moon thought about what Zora had said for a long time after she was gone. Maybe the little one is right, thought the moon to himself. 'Maybe it is time to go out and see the sky. But I don't have a broom to fly around on and if I leave my orbit I might just fall down and break into pieces.' The moon's spirits were dampened a little. 'But I'll make the most of what I have got,' said the moon determinedly, cheering himself up. 'I'll travel around on my orbit.' With that, the moon set off. And as he travelled began the phases of the moon – though he himself didn't know anything about it! When he journeyed from the other side of the earth towards the sun, he started appearing smaller and smaller – and hence shining less brightly – to the earthlings. When he was exactly between the earth and the sun after about fifteen days of travelling, those on earth experienced a pitch-dark night and were alarmed as they thought that he had disappeared. But then he appeared again and slowly started getting bigger as he travelled back to his original place. And the best part was that his shining differently every night fitted Zora's writing schedule perfectly! As Zora watched this magic from earth, she just couldn't fathom what had happened. But she was sure that the moon had something to do with it and was grateful to him for that. As for the moon, he absolutely loved this travelling. The little one had been right – it was such fun!

After this incident, Zora and the moon must have thanked each other silently in their prayers a thousand times – not knowing how much they had helped the other one as well as themselves!

A Sweet Curse

THERE was, once upon a time, a little man named Hans, who lived in a tiny town on the bank of a beautiful river. Hans had always dreamt of owning his own little café. So, after reading a lot of books on the subject and visiting all the cafés in the nearby towns, he was ready to build his very own café.

Hans first went around the town, looking for workers who would help him build the café. But the townsfolk were a lazy lot and there was not a single soul who was willing to help him. Thus Hans started off by himself. He worked day and night, digging the ground, carrying bricks and mixing cement.

When the café was built, he went around the town again, looking for people who would help him decorate the café. But the townsfolk were a lazy lot and there was still not a single soul who was willing to help him. So Hans again started off by himself. He worked day and night, building chairs and tables, sewing curtains and hanging beautiful pictures on the walls. Finally, the café was complete and what a pleasure it was to look at! The walls had been painted a rich, cream colour, the red tiles shone brightly in the sun, the doors and windows were bottle-green and sky-blue curtains, with the most delicate floral patterns, flapped lazily in the wind. There was also a green-and-white striped awning over the front door. And a few tables and chairs were set under big, blue umbrellas in the garden behind the café.

Now all Hans needed was a few cooks and waiters to help him cook and serve. He had already prepared a list of items that he intended to serve in his little café. There was to be a variety of salads, soups, sandwiches, breads, cakes, quiches, pies, waffles and lots of desserts!

Hans knew that the people in his town had proven to be a lazy lot until now. But he was sure that when they saw his lovely café they would be more than willing to work there. So Hans went around the town again, looking for people who would help him cook and serve in the café. But the townsfolk were a really lazy lot and there was not a single soul who was willing to help him. So, yet again, Hans started off by himself. He had no choice, now that he had posted advertisements about his café all over the town. He worked day and night, kneading dough, chopping vegetables and brewing coffee.

As soon as the rich aroma of the first batch of waffles and coffee wafted from the café to people's noses, the place started filling up. The folks of the town were a greedy lot and there was not a single soul who wanted to be left out. Hans had his hands full. He kept rushing from table to table, taking orders from everyone, then rushing to the kitchen, preparing the food and then rushing back to the tables – first to serve the food, then to clear the table, then to present the bill and finally to collect the money.

Hans did just fine for the first couple of days. But as the café grew in popularity and more and more people started visiting it, Hans started losing control. The tables were never cleared on time, the cakes and pies burnt because of being left in the oven for too long and he lost track of how much to charge whom. The popularity of his café went down. The number of customers visiting his café started decreasing. Business was bad.

After a particularly bad day at the café – there had been only two customers – Hans locked its front door and set off for his favourite place in town – the river bank. He often went there when he was upset and the steady flow of the water never failed to calm him. Today, as he sat on a grassy patch near the river, he had to bite his lower lip hard to keep himself from crying. In order to distract himself, he picked up a few pebbles and started throwing them into the water and observing the ripples that they created. The beautiful concentric circles that were created never failed to fascinate him and he couldn't take his eyes off them.

As he sat there, throwing pebbles, he remembered a story he had once read – about a man who finds a lamp floating in the river waters. He takes it out and starts rubbing it with a soft cloth to clean it. A genie appears from the lamp and fulfils every wish that the man has. 'I could really use such a lamp now,' Hans

muttered wistfully to himself. 'That's the only thing that can save my café now!' He had not even finished speaking when a lamp came along, drifting on the river water. Hans could hardly believe his eyes. He rubbed his eyes, pinched himself to make sure that he wasn't dreaming and then waded into the water to catch the lamp. It was a lovely brass one with intricate carvings on it. It certainly looked the type that would have a genie inside. Hans rubbed the lamp with trembling hands, scarcely being able to contain his excitement. And then it happened. A genie floated out of the lamp and hovered in front of him with his head bowed. But he didn't look ready to serve his master. Instead, he looked really doleful.

Hans was about to ask him what the matter was when the genie looked up and said, 'I know I am supposed to say "How may I serve you master?" and then grant whatever your heart wishes for. But I am really sorry. My story is a very sad one. I was sitting in my lamp, close to the river, as that is my favourite spot to relax. I was enjoying listening to the soft gushing of the waters when a strong wind blew. My lamp toppled over and fell into the river! The water entered it and washed away all my powers. I have no magic left in me now. But if there is anything else I can do, do tell me, because we genies love to help.' And the genie bowed his head again.

Hans stood there stunned. He didn't know what to say. He had already been planning on what to ask the genie for. But then a thought struck him. He said to the genie, 'I have a small café in this town and I desperately need a helping hand in there. Will you help me cook and serve?'

'I cannot cook, master, but I will definitely help you serve.' The genie looked much happier now. 'That will do, that will do.' Hans jumped with joy. 'Come, I'll show you the café.' And with that, he led the genie to the café.

'Your work will be very simple', Hans told the genie. 'All you have to do is to go to the tables and ask our customers for their order. And then simply go and fetch what they want.' 'That sounds simple enough.' The genie smiled. 'Good!' Hans smiled back. 'Then go and catch a good night's sleep now for we have a long and busy day ahead.'

That night, Hans slept peacefully after a long time. But he wouldn't have been so much at peace had he known a mistake that he had made which would cost him a lot later. He had forgotten to show the menu card to the genie and explain all the items on it to him. For the genie, who came from an entirely different world of fairies, witches, pixies and goblins who ate only the fruits and vegetables they found in the forest, had no idea what a soup or a pie was. There was going to be a lot of confusion in the café the next day!

The next day dawned bright and sunny. Hans excitedly hung the 'Open' sign in the window, tied his apron and went whistling into the kitchen. The genie hovered over the tables waiting for the customers to come. When the first guest was seated, the genie floated over to him, greeted him politely and asked him what he wanted. This guest, who was a very snobbish man, said, 'I will only have something from the French cuisine. Hmmm, let me see.' He twirled his moustache, adjusted the glasses perched on his nose and scanned the menu card. 'Ah yes, I would like a croissant please.' 'A what?' the genie asked, dumbstruck. 'A croissant, you fool! Look here', cried the man and pointed to the word on the menu card.

The genie peered at it and, in his bewilderment failed to notice the 'i' in it. 'Oh! Crossant, a cross ant,' exclaimed the genie in relief because he knew what that was. In the ant hill close to where he lived, there lived a red ant who was very cross all the time. She always had a frown on her forehead and she bit everyone who got in her way. She was hence known as the cross ant. The genie wondered why anyone would want to eat her. 'But what do I care,' he thought to himself. 'It will be good riddance to bad rubbish!' Grinning at this thought, he set off towards the ant hill. Luckily for him, the cross ant was fast asleep. He picked her up gently, floated to the café and set her on the table in front of the snobbish man.

'What in the world is this?' shrieked the man, jumping up and dancing around the table, forgetting his manners. The cross ant, whose sleep had been spoilt by the noise, became even crosser now and bit the snobbish man hard. The man flew into a rage and stormed out of the café, cursing the ant and the genie and the café. Hans was extremely upset because of this incident, but he was also secretly pleased because he had never liked the snobbish man. So he did not shout at the genie. Instead, he took the genie to the kitchen and showed him what a croissant was.

The next customer to visit the café was a pretty little girl with curly brown hair, wearing a checked pink frock. She loved all kinds of sweet food and hence wanted a brownie. 'A brownie!' exclaimed the genie in relief because he knew what that was. In a house close to where he lived stayed a little brownie. He was a small creature, a kind of a house elf, who worked in the house in exchange for food and small gifts. He was a hard-working, jolly little fellow. The genie wondered why anybody would want to eat him and he felt sad because he was rather fond of the little brownie. But as it was his duty, he set off towards the house. Luckily for him, the brownie was fast asleep. Brownies work only at night and hence sleep during the day. He picked him up gently, floated to the café and set him on the pretty little girl's table. 'Oh, he is so cute!' cried the girl, forgetting what she had ordered. The brownie was woken up by the cry and was startled to see the new surroundings. But when he saw the pretty little girl looking at him with her soft brown eyes, he couldn't help but smile at her. Hans, who had just seen what had happened, grew extremely upset with the genie's mistake and rushed to apologise to the girl. But he saw that the little girl and the brownie were happily chatting with one another and his anger mellowed a little. So he didn't shout at the genie. Instead, he took him to the kitchen and showed him what a brownie was.

The next customer to visit the café was a short, fat woman with a face like that of a pig. She ate like a pig as well. Hence Hans was very happy that he would get a large order and hoped that the genie wouldn't make any mistake now. The genie floated over to her to take her order. 'I need time to decide what I will eat,' grunted the woman. 'But until then, I'll munch on a sandwich.' 'A sandwich!' exclaimed the genie in relief because he knew what that was. On a beach close to to his home, lived the Sand Witch. He didn't know her very well. All he knew was that she was a tall, bony, hot-tempered witch with a hooked nose. She was one of the most powerful witches ever – she controlled all the sands on earth. The genie wondered why anyone would want to munch on her, but since he didn't know her personally, he didn't care much. He was only a little scared as to how he would fetch the mighty, hot-tempered witch. He was also worried that he might make a mistake again. He turned to Hans for help, but he saw that Hans was extremely busy serving the other customers. So he set off towards the beach to do his job. Luckily for him, the Sand Witch was fast asleep under a coconut tree. So he picked her up gently, floated to the café and set her on the table in front of the fat woman. The fat woman looked at the tall, bony figure and took her to be another waiter at the café. So she prodded the sleeping witch with a fat finger to wake her up. The witch woke up with a start and was very angry to see that someone had taken her away from her beautiful beach and brought her to this noisy, crowded place. And as is the property of sand, the sand that flowed in her veins heated up quickly and her anger rose. She stood tall and straight before the woman and looked at her with eyes that glinted like sand grains in the hot sun. 'Yes, please?' the Sand Witch asked with a dangerous politeness.

'What do you have for dessert?' asked the short, fat woman. 'Dessert?' repeated the witch, not knowing what that was and not caring to know either. 'I'll show you the finest dessert you have ever seen,' she said with an evil glint in her eyes. And then, with a sweep of her long, black cloak, she brought a huge, colossal wave of sand into the café. The wave was so massive, that it covered not only the café, but the entire town and many more towns around it in sand. 'The finest dessert ever!' The Sand Witch grinned, pleased with her work.

Ever since, a large mass of sand has been called a desert.

A Scoop of Trouble

ONCE upon a time, there lived a witch named Zoobi. Zoobi was the most successful children's book author that had ever lived in Witchland. She was extremely popular among the little witches and wizards of Witchland. They devoured her books as soon as she wrote them. Oh no, wait a minute. We cannot say that Zoobi wrote books because she didn't exactly write them. She didn't write stories, nor did she tell them, she ... well ... yes, she made them. That's right! Zoobi made stories, she was a story-maker. I'll explain how she did that.

Zoobi first decided what or whom she wanted the story to be about. Let's say she wanted a story about a prince, a princess and a dragon. She would then take a strand of the princess's golden hair, one tiny piece of the prince's red cape and one scale off the dragon's back. She would put all this in her big, black cauldron and then pour the story potion – which was a sweet-smelling, light violet liquid – on top of it. She would then keep stirring this mixture very slowly until she felt that the story was ready. Then she would dip sheets of plain white paper into this mixture for a minute and then take them out. And there the story would be – written on the white paper in neat, cursive handwriting, complete with pictures. And almost anything could have happened in the story. It could have been a tale where the prince rescues the princess from the dragon. Or it could have been a tale in which the princess falls in love with the dragon and kills the prince who tries to attack the dragon. Or the prince and princess could be friends who have a pet dragon that they ride on. And these are the simplest examples that I could think of. Often the stories were filled with hundreds of things – princesses, pixies, rabbits, shoes, crystal balls, zebras, stars, apples, the sea, spiders, a magic lamp – you just name it! Sometimes Zoobi decided beforehand what type of story she wanted and then added a potion accordingly – a red rose for a love story, a bubbly blue for a funny story and a deep black for a tragedy. But, most of the time, Zoobi didn't add any such potion and let the story take on any form that it wanted.

As I said before, Zoobi's stories were extremely popular in Witchland. The witches and wizards just couldn't get enough of them. So they were constantly in demand. And Zoobi became a very busy witch. She got herself two helpers. One of them was Cric, the crab. Cric was a glossy red colour. He was a simple, kind-hearted fellow who was very sincere in his work. Zoobi needed him to stir the story mixtures. She had to constantly travel all over Witchland to collect ingredients for her next story. So she needed someone to stir the story that was already bubbling away in her cauldron. Cric would sit on the rim of the black cauldron and stir the mixture with a thin, silver rod. There was one more advantage of having Cric around. If Zoobi suddenly felt that she didn't want a particular thing to be in the story anymore, Cric would reach into the cauldron and gently take out that ingredient with his pincers, without disturbing the rest of the mixture.

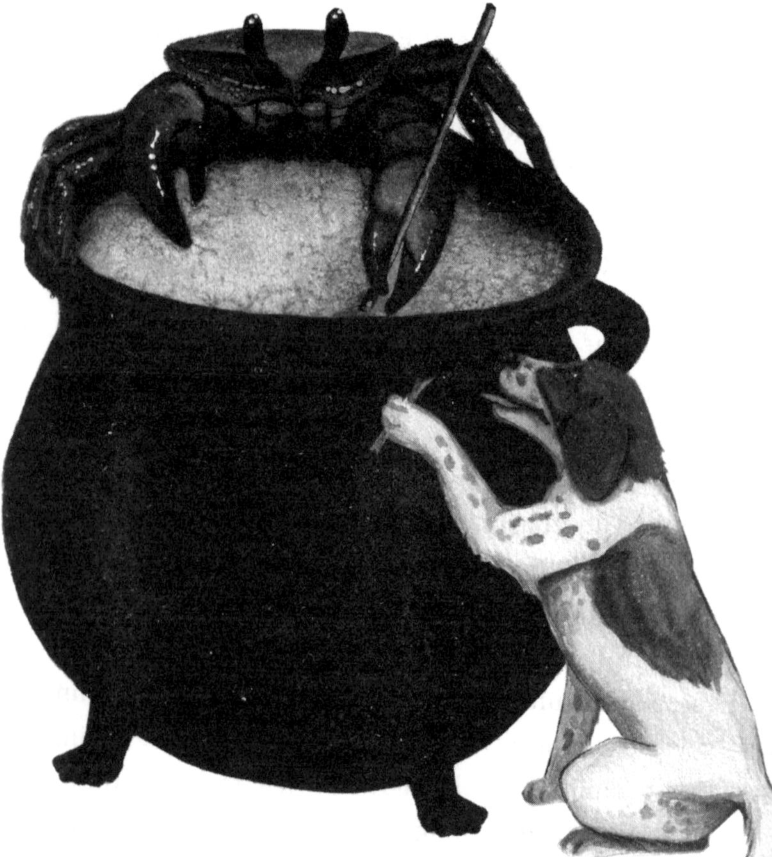

The other helper was Scoop, the dog. He was one of the cutest little dogs you would ever see. He was a cuddly fellow with the softest, velvet-brown eyes and had a soft coat of brown-and-white patches. When Zoobi had gone to fetch him, he had just been a newly born puppy who had curled himself up into a ball and was fast asleep. Zoobi had thought that he looked just like a scoop of chocolate and vanilla ice-cream and had hence named him 'Scoop'. But all of Scoop's cuteness was limited only to his looks. In reality, he was just a big scoop of trouble. Zoobi had got him to help her with collecting ingredients. She required a variety of ingredients from different places and it wasn't possible for her to go to all these places herself. Plus, she often had to be at home to dip the papers into her story mix. So she used to give Scoop a list of ingredients and send him out ingredient hunting. Now Scoop was a really meddlesome fellow who just couldn't mind his own business. Maybe he didn't mean to be troublesome, but he was simply too curious for anyone's good. When he was out ingredient-hunting, he always stopped to chat with anyone he met on the way. He tapped the rosebuds and asked them to open up quickly because he was impatient to see how they would look once they had bloomed fully. He chased the lambs all around the grassy meadows and kept begging the bees for a taste of their honey.

Once Zoobi had to go away to attend her great-aunt's hundredth birthday. This great-aunt lived very far away, in one of the remote corners of Witchland, so it would take Zoobi quite some time to fly there and back. She would be gone for a whole day. But she wasn't going to let her work suffer. So she put some ingredients into her cauldron, poured the light violet potion over it and looked at it for a while. Yes, this was going to be a good story, she didn't need to stay around to see whether the patterns in it were forming well. Cric just had to keep stirring it and the story would be ready even before she got back. She would just have to dip the papers into it once she was back. She then told Cric to stir the mixture well, gave Scoop a new list of ingredients, kissed them both goodbye and flew away on her broomstick.

Scoop was sad to see his mistress go for he loved her very much. But at the same time, his doggy heart was leaping with joy. Now was the chance to make his dearest wish come true. His dearest wish was to be part of one of Zoobi's stories. He loved to imagine how he would be in a story – maybe a strong, brave dog that saves the world or even a dog that belongs to a king. The king would give him a golden crown to wear, a silken cushion to sit on and pamper him silly with all kinds of goodies. 'Now I will know!' Scoop chuckled to himself, rubbing his paws gleefully. As soon as Zoobi was out of sight, he plucked one of his hairs and went to Cric. 'Here,' he said, 'put my hair into the story mix, I want to be part of the story too.'

'Are you out of your mind?' cried Cric. 'Zoobi will be furious when she finds out what you did!' 'Oh no, there's absolutely no need to worry about that,' Scoop reassured his friend. 'You see, this story is meant to be about a dog. I know, because yesterday all that was on my list was "a dog hair". And I am a dog, right? So why not put in my hair?' Cric didn't seem very convinced. 'I think it would be better to take Zoobi's permission first,' he said. 'What if she doesn't allow it, Cric? Then I'll never be part of a story,' said Scoop and looked at Cric with his soft, velvety-brown eyes that were enough to melt the heart of the toughest crab. 'All right, I'll do it because you are my friend,' said Cric, taking the hair and dropping it into the mixture.

Scoop happily licked Cric's face as a 'thank you' gesture and set off ingredient-hunting. But no sooner was he out of the house than a thought struck him. He quickly came bounding inside. 'Cric!' he shouted. 'I gave you one of my white hairs. So will that mean that I will be a white dog in the story? I won't like that – I want my brown patches too.' And before Cric could say anything, Scoop had plucked out a brown hair and was holding it out to Cric. Cric was going to refuse, but the soft, velvety-brown eyes did their magic again. Cric had just put in the brown hair when another thought struck Scoop. 'Both the hairs that I gave you were from my tummy,' he said. 'So does that mean that I won't have a head, back, tail, ears or paws in the story? I won't like that.' And before Cric could say anything Scoop had plucked out hairs from all over his body. And the simple, kind-hearted Cric just couldn't say no. As a result, twenty-one hairs of Scoop found their way into the cauldron.

To understand the consequences of Scoop's actions, one must know the laws of story-making. If Scoop had dropped just one hair of his into the mixture, the story would have been about any dog – at the most, maybe a dog that is brown-and-white. But the more hairs one puts in, the stronger the effect becomes. So the dog in this particular story would, with the number of hairs put, become more and more like Scoop himself. And little did Scoop know that the story was to be just about a witch and her pet dog. And the witch was to be quite like Zoobi, for Zoobi had put in five strands of her own black hair. So the story that Cric was stirring right now was a story of Zoobi and Scoop!

Zoobi dipped sheets of plain white paper into the mixture as soon as she came back that night. The story that emerged on the paper was that of a witch who was a story-maker and of her nosy, meddlesome pet dog who once dropped his own hair into the story mixture. Zoobi knew instantly what had happened. She wasn't angry, but she was quite disappointed with Scoop. 'If you wanted to become part of a story so badly, Scoop, you should have just told it to me. I would have dropped your hair in it myself,' she scolded him. 'But now I can never trust you anywhere near my story-making cauldron.' So, henceforth, poor Scoop had to live in a kennel in the garden outside the house.

The young witches and wizards who read this story understood what must have happened and they naturally started feeling that dogs were very meddlesome creatures. So it would be a real headache to have them as pets. When they grew up, they thus kept pet cats instead of pet dogs. And cats proved to be really good pets. ('Because they are too lazy to be any trouble,' said Zischka with a wink. 'They just about do the work that they are given and then spend the rest of the time sleeping.')

Whatever the reason, ever since the Scoop incident, witches have always had pet cats – and black ones, for black is a witch's favourite colour.

– Mischka, the Cat

'Good' Witches

THERE lived, once upon a time, in Witchland a witch named Helga. Helga was nothing like what a good witch should be. For starters, she didn't look like a witch at all – she was short and plump instead of being tall and bony. Her hair was silky and not rough and her nose was not long and crooked, but was small and round like a button. And more importantly, she didn't behave like a good witch should. There had been a time when she had at least acted like the other witches. But all of it had changed the day Helga visited a city where humans lived. She was supposed to be collecting certain ingredients for

a potion, which are found only in the rubbish bins of humans. But once there, a big half-torn book caught her eye. It was a book of recipes. Helga scanned the first few pages and was mesmerised. She had no idea that one could cook such delicious-looking things from the fruits and vegetables that one saw every day. She forgot what she had come for in the first place and continued reading the recipes. Even as she flew back on her broom, her eyes were glued to the colourful pictures on the pages. Once back home, she was determined to try out every recipe in the book and then make some of her own!

The book said that the key to good taste was to 'keep it natural'. No food processors and none of that instant noodle stuff – whatever these things were – one should use freshly picked vegetables and grind the spices at home. 'Keep it natural!' repeated Helga to herself and threw away her potions and spell books. And from now on, her broom would only be used to sweep the kitchen floor and her big, black cauldron would only be used to cook the most delicious soups and stews.

Helga stopped using magic altogether. Now all she could think of was cooking. She had also shooed away her pet black cat, fearing that his hair would fall into the food and spoil it. All the other witches watched this turn of events first with astonishment and then with anger. Helga wasn't being a good witch! Whenever you passed her house, she would be bustling about in the kitchen wearing an apron – peeling, chopping, frying and stirring something in her cauldron that didn't smell like a potion! Slowly, the other witches stopped talking to Helga. And if they did speak, it was only in the form of taunts. The only one who supported Helga through all this was her husband – Hob, the wizard. He loved to eat what his wife cooked and he always encouraged her to try out new dishes. So Helga made tomato soup, vegetable dumplings, potato salad, cheese macaroni, apple pies, mushroom pasta, gingerbread, blueberry muffins, corn patties, chocolate-chip cookies, lemon tarts and – oh, the list is endless! Helga kept cooking and both of them kept eating. And they kept getting rounder and fatter.

Hence, it was no wonder that when three years later, Helga gave birth to three baby witches, they were all round and fat. They had the chubbiest little cheeks, the silkiest hair and noses just like their mother's. And it was also no surprise that Helga named her babies after her three current favourite ingredients: the eldest one was Soya, the middle one was named Tami – short for tamarind – and the youngest was Mayo – short for mayonnaise. When the three little witches started going to school, they were teased endlessly by the other witches and wizards because of the way they looked and because of their silly names. The poor witches used to come home crying every day. They started doing everything that they could in order to look like normal witches. They stopped washing and brushing their hair so that it would lose its silkiness, they pulled and twisted each other's noses to make them long and crooked. And instead of flying on their broomsticks to school, they ran to school and back home so that they would become thinner and bonier. But all their efforts were in vain. They looked just as they had before and the teasing continued.

One night, the three sisters lay in bed, unable to go to sleep. They had had another day of unending teasing and taunting. Mayo had cried so much that her eyes were red and sore. The sisters were exhausted, but they still couldn't sleep. A rich aroma of coffee and cupcakes drifted to their noses from the kitchen below. 'Why is our mother like this?' sighed Tami. 'I mean, she's a dear and I love her so, but ... but I just wish she was a bit more like the other witches.' 'I love her too and I hate to say this, but our mother is a disgrace to witchkind,' said Soya, who was never one to mince her words. 'And if we don't do something about it soon, we will be declared outcastes.' 'Can't we just fly away?' asked Mayo mournfully, rubbing her tired eyes. 'Somewhere far, far away from Witchland. Maybe to a land where there are no mirrors. I can't bear to look at myself anymore!' Mayo started crying again, remembering how Wozo, a wizard in her class, had spread the rumour that Mayo was actually bald and that the silkworms had made her a wig of silk. And that she came running to school because she didn't know how to fly a broomstick. Which was a good thing, because if she ever sat on one, it would break into two under her weight. Little wizards could be really cruel!

Tami got up from her bed, came to Mayo and hugged her tightly, trying to stop her sobs. Soya, who was still lying on her bed, spoke slowly, staring up at the ceiling, 'I don't think all this has got to do anything with looks. Our mother has always looked the way she has. But there was a time when she was accepted by the other witches. But then she started acting all weird. She kept cooking all the time and refused to use any magic. That's when the other witches stopped talking to her.' A pin-drop silence hung in the room for a few minutes. Then Soya suddenly sat up in her bed and said, 'I know what we have to do. We cannot help how we look anymore. We tried to do everything we could to change it, but that didn't work. We have been chasing the wrong goal all along. What we need to do is to change our behaviour. We have to act like witches.' Soya stopped after this long speech to catch her breath. Tami and Mayo stared at her for a moment. Then Tami nodded her head. 'Yes, I think you are right, Soya, we should train ourselves to become the most perfect witches that there ever were. What say, Mayo?' She turned to look at her younger sister, who was pulling her tiny little nose. 'I don't know,' she said dolefully. 'What if that doesn't work? I still think flying away is a better idea.'

'Don't be such a coward, Mayo!' Soya said sharply, but bit her tongue when she saw tears welling up in Mayo's eyes. 'Think about it, Mayo,' she said, her voice softening a little. 'If you become a good witch who knows her spells, you could turn that stupid Wozo into a toad or a worm!' Mayo couldn't help giggling at this thought and her eyes started twinkling. And with that, the three sisters huddled close together and started chalking out a plan to become 'good witches'.

Soya, Tami and Mayo began implementing their plan the very next day. They started flying to school on their broomsticks. They went to the market and bought themselves three shiny, black cauldrons with the pocket money that they had saved up. And they swore that they would use it only to prepare potions. They also adopted a black kitten each. These kittens, however, were denied entry into the house by Helga and had to, hence, live in the garden. But the most important thing that the three witches did, and rightly so, was to start paying careful attention in school, especially in the classes for potions and spells. Because making the perfect potion and casting the perfect spell is the true hallmark of a good witch. The sisters spent hours in the school library, devouring as many books on magic as they could. And once home, they burnt the midnight oil practising the art of potion-making. Their hard work paid off. They passed all their exams with good grades and, on the last day of school, the principal declared them to be the finest students the school had ever produced.

But more importantly, Soya, Tami and Mayo – with their persistence and hard work – had earned the respect of their fellow witches and wizards. However, all this was not enough for the sisters. They wanted to prove to Witchland that it wasn't just by fluke or only by hard work that they could cast such wonderful spells. It was true witch blood that ran through their veins. They wanted to help witches and wizards and other beings with their spells and potions because that's what witches are for. And they wanted to do something spectacular that would make everyone sit up and take notice of the family that had been ridiculed for so long. After a lot of debates and discussions at home, it was decided that each sister would set up a little 'office' in town. This office would be open to anyone and everyone. Anybody who needed any kind of help could come to any one of the three sisters and she would help using her spells and potions, without taking anything in return.

And so the three sisters set up their offices in town. They were small cottages, well-stocked with everything a witch would ever need. In the centre

stood a giant-sized, black cauldron. All around it were tiny, black cauldrons with some liquid already bubbling inside and small, neatly labelled bottles stacked onto shelves containing all the possible ingredients that one could need for a potion.

On the first day, the three sisters sat in their respective offices, waiting for someone to come along. Soon, there was a small knock on Soya's door. Soya got up in a second, rushed to the door and flung it open. Outside the door stood a small pixie, wearing a green tunic, red shoes and a white hat with red polka dots on it. A tiny bell tinkled on the top of the hat. He gave Soya a bright smile and held out a tiny hand. 'Hello, I am Pix, the pixie.' Soya shook his hand warmly, ushered him into her office and offered him a chair to sit on. 'Tell me, Pix, how may I help you?' Soya asked, coming straight to the point. 'I have come to ask you for something. But before that, I'll have to tell you my story, which, I'm afraid, is a bit long. So be patient, dear witch,' said Pix and began his story.

'You see, I work for Princess Penelope. Princess Penelope lives in a huge, magnificent palace. The palace is unlike any other palace that you might have seen. It is not a square or rectangular building.

It is round because it has been built on the shores of a round lake. The palace encircles the lake completely. And between the palace and the lake is a garden, which is also circular, of course. The palace gardeners have worked very hard and made the garden one of the most beautiful ones ever. The soft, green grass is always very neatly trimmed and the most beautiful flowers bloom there – the reddest roses, the whitest jasmines, the pinkest lilies and the orangest marigolds.' Pix paused to breathe and then continued. 'Now, if there is one thing that Princess Penelope loves with all her heart, it is to dance. She herself is a very graceful dancer and is always looking for an opportunity to dance. But there are very few dance parties and balls organised around where we live. So, a few days ago, Princess Penelope decided to throw a ball every Sunday evening and invite all the princes and princesses of the neighbouring lands to it. And what better place to host the ball than her very own garden! The soft, green grass would caress the delicate feet of the princesses and the rich scent of the flowers would entrance everyone and make them want to keep on dancing. The first ball was to be held last Sunday.

'But there was a little problem. Since the ball was to begin after sunset, the garden would be dark. Hence, Princess Penelope called a group of goblins and had them make light arrangements in the garden. These goblins set up lamps in the entire garden. I must tell you what kind of lamps they were. They had been made by fixing a candle on the top of a very tall wooden pole. Once the goblins were done with their work, they called me and told me that they would be going now and that I – Pix, the pixie – would be in charge of the lights henceforth. It is very simple, they said, all you have to do is to light the candles before the ball begins. And then they scooted off. I looked at the lamps in dismay. They were three times taller than me. How was I to reach the candles? But me, I am not one to cry. Pix, the pixie, is a cheery sort. I started my job two hours before sunset this Sunday. I lit a small bonfire in the garden. Then I took a long wooden stick and dipped it into the fire so that its tip was lit. And then I ran around the garden lighting all the lamps. But it took me so much longer than I had expected. The candles kept blowing out because of the silly wind who had come uninvited to the ball.' Pix crinkled his nose disapprovingly. 'No sooner had I lit one candle than the candle ten poles earlier would go out. So, all through the evening, I kept running round and round the garden, trying to keep the candles burning. The bell on my hat tinkled like crazy and my head felt all dizzy.' Pix stopped. He was panting, as if he'd just finished running. Soya could almost see Pix running around the garden with his bell tinkling. This picture was so funny that she wanted to laugh, but she controlled herself just in time. 'My dear witch,' Pix spoke again, 'please help me. If I faint running around the garden like this, the candles will remain unlit and I will lose my job. There are one thousand and one candles in all!' Pix was almost in tears now. Soya felt extremely sorry for the pixie and felt guilty about wanting to laugh earlier. She immediately made up her mind to do everything she could to help Pix.

'Don't worry, Pix', said Soya softly, patting his hand. 'I'll find a solution to your problems. In fact, I think I already have an idea. I need a little help from you, though. You have to go back to the garden and get me the following things: one piece of your wooden stick, a little wax from the melted candles and the ashes from your bonfire.' 'Right away!' cried Pix and sped off, his golden bell tinkling. He soon brought Soya whatever she had asked for and then Soya started working. She put the piece of wood, the wax and the ash into her cauldron and then poured a sizzling-hot red-and-orange liquid on top. As soon as the burning liquid touched the ingredients, they caught fire. Bright red-and-orange flames shot up from the cauldron. Into this crackling fire, Soya dropped a round, white pebble and then she sat patiently by the side. After the fire had died out, she dipped her hand into the cauldron and brought out the pebble, which was now shiny bright. She handed it to the pixie and said, 'Here you go, Pix. This is the solution to your problem. Now all you have to do is to hold this in one hand and press it with the thumb of the other. And within a second, all your one thousand and one candles will be lit!'

Pix looked at her with eyes that were as shiny and bright as the pebble. 'Thank you, thank you, thank you, dear witch!' he cried. 'You are most welcome, Pix.' Soya winked at him. Pix stared at the pebble for a while. Then he looked up at Soya and asked her curiously, 'What is this called?' Soya was taken aback. She hadn't expected this question. She didn't know what to say because even she didn't know what it was called. It didn't have a name because nothing of that sort had existed before.

I have created something new and I can name it whatever I wish to, Soya realised with a beating heart. 'What do I name it?' Soya muttered to herself. 'Witches always name their spells after themselves. So, to be a good witch, I must do the same. But Soya is such a ridiculous name! I'll just take my initial "S" and add to it "witch". That will show everyone that being a witch is more important to me. Yes! S.Witch it will be!' Soya exclaimed, liking her decision. She smiled at Pix and said, 'Switch. This is a switch.' 'A switch to light my one thousand and one candles!' Pix laughed and ran off, eagerly awaiting the next ball. And so ended the first success story.

Now it was Tami's turn to do some magic. She was sitting in her office a few days later, reading a book on spells when she heard a very soft, shy knock on the door. She shut her book quickly, rushed to the door and flung it open. But imagine her surprise when she saw no one at the door! She looked all around in bewilderment, but there was not a single soul in sight. She was about to go back inside when she heard a soft rustle of leaves. She turned around and saw that the bush in front of her office was moving slightly. She went to the bush and gently parted its leaves. And she saw that in the middle of the bush sat a small rabbit. It was pure white in colour and had curled itself up. If it wasn't for the floppy ears, Tami would have mistaken it to be a ball of cotton. The rabbit had shut its eyes tightly and was quivering. 'Hey, little bunny,' Tami spoke as gently as she could. The rabbit opened its eyes and then shut them immediately. 'Was it you who knocked on the door?' Tami asked. The rabbit nodded, its eyes still shut. 'Then why are you sitting here? Come on inside!' Tami said. 'I am scared,' the rabbit said. 'Of what?' asked Tami in surprise, but she received no answer. 'Okay,' Tami said, 'I am going back in now. But I'll leave the door open, just in case.' And with that, she returned inside.

After a little while, the rabbit hopped in softly. 'Hello, witch', he said, mustering up all his courage. 'I am Scoot, the bunny, and I need your help.' 'Of course, Scoot!' said Tami. 'Go on, tell me what can I do for you?' 'I have to tell you something about myself,' began the bunny. 'I get scared very easily. In fact, I feel scared all the time.' 'As if one doesn't notice that straight away!' Tami chuckled to herself, but didn't say anything out loud. 'I ... I ... please help me!' ended the bunny abruptly. 'What are you so scared of?' Tami asked curiously. 'Oh, everything,' replied the bunny. 'Even if a tiny raindrop falls on the ground, I get scared and scoot off. That's why they call me Scoot.' He paused for a while before continuing. 'But I'm most scared of the lion, the tiger, the wolf and the fox!' he cried indignantly. He sounded like a little wizard in school who is complaining about the bullies troubling him to the headmaster. Tami couldn't help smiling. 'Don't smile!' cried Scoot. 'They are baddies who are always looking for me, trying to catch me and eat me.' Scoot's ears quivered with a mixture of fear and anger. 'But all you have to do is to run away when you know they are coming. Rabbits can run very fast, can't they?' Tami said. 'That's the problem,' Scoot said unhappily. 'I never know when they are coming. They come sneaking through the tall grass so that I don't see them.' 'Can't you smell them?' enquired Tami. 'No,' said Scoot sadly. 'My nose is a bad nose.' 'I know how it is not to like your nose,' said Tami. 'But don't worry, Scoot, I'll cast a spell and make your troubles go away. So cheer up! Hop home for now and come back tomorrow evening. I'll have my spell ready then.'

So Scoot scooted off and Tami got to work. She worked in her office for a little while and when night crept in, she crept out to the forest. One by one, she sneaked up to the lion, the tiger, the wolf and the fox and plucked one hair from each of them. She even captured their smell in four tiny glass bottles that she had carried with her. Then she tiptoed back home. The next day in her office, she emptied the smells from the glass bottles, along with the hairs, into a big, black cauldron. She then poured a frothy blue potion on top, which caused the ingredients in the cauldron to move about rapidly. She then waited patiently till the moving stopped and all the ingredients were completely dissolved in the potion. After this, she waited for Scoot to arrive.

As soon as evening fell, Scoot hopped into her office once again. 'Come here,' said Tami, who was standing next to the cauldron. Scoot hopped over obediently. Tami sat down on her knees in front of him and dipped a finger into the frothy blue potion. She drew out her finger and tapped it three times on the bunny's nose. Both of them sat still in silence for a while. And then Scoot's nose started moving rapidly with tiny little jerks. 'Hey, hey, what is happening to me?' cried Scoot. He was very scared now and wanted to scoot off. But Tami caught his tail just in time. 'Just wait a minute, Scoot,' she said. 'Tell me, do you smell anything?' Scoot concentrated for a second. 'Yes, yes, I ... I smell something. I smell a fox!' he yelled. His eyes widened in horror and his whole body trembled. 'You are right,' Tami exclaimed 'there is indeed a fox outside. Look out of the window.' And sure enough, far away in a field, Scoot could see a fox. A very scared Scoot jumped into an empty cauldron and sat there with his eyes tightly closed. 'Come out, Scoot!' Tami said. 'You have no reason to be afraid – the fox is too far off. He won't know you are here. Don't you see you can smell him even when he is so far away? Similarly, you can smell a lion, tiger and a wolf. Your rapidly moving nose will smell them so that you can run away in time.' Scoot jumped out of the cauldron and smiled for the first time that day.

'What a great gift you have given me, dear witch. Many bunny thanks to you! But what is this that my nose does?' And Tami knew that it was time to name the newest spell in Witchland. But she had already decided what that name would be – she was going to follow Soya's way and use her initial 'T' and 'witch'.

So 'T.witch' it would be! 'Twitch,' said Tami to Scoot. 'Your nose twitches.' 'My nose twitches' repeated Scoot happily. 'And see how cute it makes you look!' Tami held a mirror in front of him. Scoot had never been called cute by any female before, so he suddenly felt shy. He just gave Tami a quick hug and hopped away, his nose twitching merrily. The second success story was complete.

Yes, now it was Mayo's turn. And Mayo could hardly wait. She couldn't wait to see who would come to her office seeking her help. She couldn't wait to emulate her sisters' successes and, most of all, she couldn't wait to create something entirely new to the world. And she already knew what that something new would be called – M.Witch! She already had a bottle labelled 'mwitch' ready on her shelf – to keep mwitch, whatever it would be! So impatient was Mayo that she left her door open and kept pacing back and forth in her office. Occasionally, she would stand at the door and look around, trying to see who was approaching her door. A few days later, as she was standing at the door like this, she saw a big black-and-white giant panda ambling slowly towards her office. When he saw Mayo standing at the door, he greeted her in a jolly manner, waving at her with his big paws. 'Hallo, little witch! He shouted out loud, 'I am Jojo, the giant panda, and I need your help.' 'I would be more than happy to help you Jojo,' Mayo said, smiling at him. 'Come on in,' she said, stepping inside her office. She then waited – impatiently, but not showing it – for the giant panda, who really was giant-sized, to squeeze himself through the door and get in. She quickly offered him a large armchair and said, 'Tell me, Jojo, how can I help you?'

The giant panda seemed to have suddenly lost all his jolliness. His big, black eyes looked infinitely sad as he sat hunched on the big armchair. He sat like this for a while and then said, 'My story is a tragedy, little witch. I work in a zoo. It is a really nice zoo – not like those where animals are kept shut in horrible cages, but one where the animals can roam around freely, playing with the children who come to visit. The children really look forward to meeting me – they are not scared of me like they are of the lion or the tiger. In fact, when they see me, their faces brighten up instantly because I remind them of their teddy bears at home. "He looks so cute and cuddly!" they cry out and rush towards me to give me a hug. And then they hug me. And then ... then ... then they don't like me anymore,' finished Jojo abruptly and burst into tears. 'What do you mean?' asked Mayo, totally surprised and confused. 'Why don't they like you anymore?' Jojo didn't answer. He just sat there and stared down at his paws. 'It must be so nice to hug a big, soft panda like you,' said Mayo. Jojo smiled sadly. 'That's what everyone thinks – a panda must be really soft. But the truth is that a panda's hair is extremely coarse and rough. Feel it for yourself', Jojo said, extending a paw. Mayo touched it. Jojo was right – it really was rough. 'My fur hurts the delicate hands and cheeks of the children,' said Jojo and started crying again. 'Please help me!'

'Don't worry, Jojo,' Mayo comforted him, patting his rough paw. 'I'm sure we can find a remedy. In fact, my brain has already started working. You go back for now and come again tomorrow evening. No, actually, you don't have to wait for that long. Come as soon as the dawn breaks. I'll work the entire night and have a spell ready for you.' So Jojo ambled back to the zoo and Mayo set to work. She consulted her spell books for a while and then prepared a list of ingredients that she would need: aloe vera, rose petals and almonds. By the time she had prepared the list she was quite tired and sleepy. But she was still impatient. She couldn't wait to finish her spell and show it off to all of Witchland. So she put on her black, pointed hat and set off towards the forest. She quickly gathered whatever she needed and then hurried back to her office. She threw everything that she had got into her black cauldron and then added a lot of cold cream and a light pink potion to it. She stirred this mixture till the break of dawn and, just before Jojo arrived, she poured it proudly into the glass bottle labelled 'mwitch'.

'Here, Jojo, I have prepared a lotion for you,' she said, handing over the bottle to him. 'Just apply it all over your body and then see how soft your fur becomes!' Jojo did as was told. And then something strange happened. Jojo started scratching himself all over – he scratched his stomach, his ears, his back and his paws. 'What's ... what's happening?' Mayo asked, full of concern. 'I ... I feel weird ... I feel like scratching myself all over,' replied Jojo. 'Oh, dearie me! What have I done?' cried a scared Mayo. She just didn't understand what had happened. 'This lotion is terrible,' screamed Jojo, throwing the bottle at Mayo.

'Now the children will never, ever like me. What have you done? Never in my life will I come to a witch again for help.' And with that, he went off, still scratching himself and cursing witches.

Mayo stood stunned for a second. Then she burst into tears. Her sobs grew louder and louder. Her sisters, who were sitting in their offices next door, heard Mayo's howling and rushed to her. 'What on earth is the matter, Mayo?' they asked. In between sobs, Mayo somehow managed to tell them what had happened. 'I don't understand this,' said Tami. 'Me too,' said Soya. 'Seems to me that you used all the right ingredients. What went wrong then?' Nobody spoke for a while. It was only Mayo's sobs that broke the silence. Then, suddenly, as if struck by some idea, Soya walked over to Mayo's cauldron. She peered inside and started inspecting the remnants of the ingredients. 'Here's what went wrong!' she exclaimed suddenly, pulling out something from the cauldron. It was a nettle – a prickly little plant. 'How did that get there?' Mayo asked, surprised. 'Maybe you got it along by mistake along with the other ingredients,' suggested Soya. 'I might have,' said Mayo slowly. 'Yes, you are right. There were a lot of nettles around the rose bush. I remember because some of them stung me.' 'Oh so that's why the panda was scratching himself so much!' Tami put two and two together. Nobody said anything for a while.

'What a fool I am!' cried Mayo, smacking herself on her forehead. She was really angry with herself now. 'It is okay, little sis, everyone makes mistakes,' said Tami, patting Mayo's head. 'I hate this thing!' cried Mayo, shaking the glass bottle. 'And I don't want to name it mwitch! I don't want my name, my initial attached to this disgusting thing.' Saying this, she rubbed off the 'M' on the label. 'And it shouldn't be a disgrace to witchkind, so I'll rub off the "witch" too!' And she started to rub it, but Soya put a hand on her shoulder and said, 'You can't rub off the entire thing Mayo, because it was after all a witch who created it.' 'Okay' sighed Mayo and stopped, but she had already rubbed off the 'w' by then. So 'itch' it was! And from that day on, when anybody feels like scratching themselves, they say that their body 'itches'.

Do you want to know what happened to Mayo later? Just hop on to the next story!

Mayo

THE spells that Soya and Tami had cast had become smashing successes in Witchland. Everyone kept talking about switches and twitching and they kept congratulating the two sisters, telling them what splendid spells they had cast and how they had made all of witchkind proud. Soya and Tami had become stars overnight. Everyone seemed to have forgotten how much they had criticised Helga and her family earlier. In fact, now that Soya and Tami were stars, the people of Witchland adored everything about them. They loved their silky hair and their chubby cheeks and their button-like noses. And now every witch and wizard felt this sudden desire to go and taste what Helga cooked. 'We have always admired you Helga,' they said. 'It takes great courage to do something different.' And Helga, the simple-minded sweetheart that she was, said nothing to them and fed them her delicious delicacies. And so good was her food that the witches and wizards were left licking their long, bony fingers. The number of hungry visitors at Helga's house increased so much that she put out a few tables and chairs in the garden for them and, before she knew it, she was running a full-fledged café.

Poor Mayo was the only one who was not doing so well. She still couldn't get over her failed spell. It was as if that 'itch' kept itching her. She felt angry with herself, sorry for herself, disappointed in herself. How *could* she have made such a mistake? If Mayo had looked around a bit, she would have seen that witches make mistakes all the time. It doesn't happen always that a witch hits upon the right spell the very first time. It is often a long process of trial and error. Often, a witch has to keep mixing different ingredients in different proportions until she gets the perfect potion. But the tears in Mayo's eyes didn't let her see anything. Her sisters tried to console her the best they could, but it didn't work. Even Jojo, the giant panda, came to visit Mayo once. He said that the itching had stopped now and that he was sorry that he had yelled at Mayo. He knew she hadn't done it on purpose. Everyone makes mistakes, right? Witches included! So he forgave her. But Mayo couldn't forgive herself. She said she couldn't bear to show her face in Witchland anymore and that she really was flying away this time. But so upset was Mayo that she forgot to take her broomstick. So she ran away. She ran as fast as her chubby legs could carry her. She ran into the heart of the deep, dark forest till her legs could carry her no more. She sat down in the middle of the forest and decided to live there. But all she did there was cry, sleep and eat the wild fruits that grew around her.

A week went by and then Mayo started feeling very homesick. She missed her sisters and her parents and her house and her pet black cat. And she felt that running away like this had been a very silly idea indeed. So she started on her way back. Her dear sisters were the first ones that she wanted to meet. So she went directly to their offices. But their doors were locked. After asking around a bit she came to know that they had gone away for some work. Soya and Tami were in great demand now! Someone or the other constantly came to them asking for help. Right now, Soya had gone with Pix to help Princess Penelope and Tami had gone with Scoot to help his bunny friends. They wouldn't be returning for quite a few days. Utterly dejected, Mayo started off towards her home. She went in and threw herself on a chair in the kitchen. Her mother, who was working in the kitchen, was pleasantly surprised to see her come in suddenly like this. And shocked too, for Mayo looked extremely tired and worn out. But Helga knew the remedy for this. She didn't say a word to Mayo. She took out a freshly baked chocolate cake from the oven, generously cut a large slice from it and gave it to Mayo. Mayo bit into the soft, warm, chocolatey cake, which melted instantly in her mouth, and she didn't know why, but somehow she just started smiling. She couldn't remember when she had felt so happy before. She didn't say anything – her mouth was too full for that – but she shot a grateful glance at her mother. Helga then fed her daughter some more and then the duo settled down for a nice, long chat over steaming mugs of coffee. The sisters had been so busy pursuing their dreams that they had hardly got a chance to bond with their mother. But now Mayo was pouring her heart out to her mother.

'Can I ask you something, my child?' Helga suddenly asked. 'Why did you set up that office?' 'I wanted to make a spell that would make everybody stop and stare. But ... but I wanted to help others too.' 'So when you were collecting the ingredients and making the potion, all you were thinking of was how to help the panda?' Mayo didn't say anything. Her face was tomato-red. 'No, Mama', she said in a voice that was so low that Helga could hardly hear her. 'I was just thinking what a splendid spell I would soon cast and how I would name it "mwitch".' 'It seems to me, Mayo, that your heart wasn't in it. You weren't enjoying what you were doing and no good work comes out of that. But you should forgive yourself now and try to find what you truly love.' And with that, Helga went out into the garden to arrange the tables and chairs for the evening.

Mayo found what she loved sooner than she had expected. She had decided to help her mother in the café till she figured out what to do next, but she soon realised that she was every bit her mother's daughter, for she too loved to cook. She was most happy when she was in the kitchen – bustling about in an apron, kneading the dough and listening to the vegetables sizzling in the frying pan. And now, thanks to Mayo's involvement, the café was doing even better than before. It was always packed.

Once, Mayo was pouring maple syrup on a fresh hot batch of waffles when her mother came in and told her to take some out to a wizard who had just ordered them. So Mayo placed some waffles in a dish and carried it out into the garden. But she suddenly stopped in her tracks. The wizard sitting at the table in front of her was so handsome! He was very tall and slim and had a long, sharp nose and curly black hair. He was sitting very comfortably in his chair, leaning back a little and looking up at the sky. His already bright blue eyes shone brighter because of the hot sun as he tapped on the table with his long, bony fingers and whistled a merry tune. Mayo's heart started beating painfully and her cheeks became hot and red. She went up to him slowly and put the waffles in front of him with trembling hands. 'Here you go,' she managed to mutter. And then, suddenly, the wizard cried out, 'Why, if it isn't our dear fatty!' Mayo looked up upon hearing this strangely familiar voice. And then it struck her. 'Wozo!' she shouted out loud, causing all the wizards and the witches in the café to look up from their plates. She knew who this wizard was! He was Wozo – her much-hated enemy from school, her classmate who had caused her so much grief by teasing her and spreading mean rumours about her. 'Bingo!' cried the wizard as he jumped to his feet and bowed gracefully. 'Wozo at your service!' Mayo stood stunned for a moment. She didn't know how to react. Painful memories from school suddenly stabbed at her heart as she remembered how much she'd cried because of this wizard. But the wizard who was standing in front of her now seemed to be a changed one. She had to admit to herself that there had been no spite in his voice when he had called her 'fatty' just now. Rather, it had been quite affectionate. And he was so good-looking!

A totally confused Mayo just spun around and rushed inside the house. Upon entering the kitchen, she saw her mother standing near the sink, washing some bowls and spoons. I should ask my mother about Wozo, thought Mayo. There were certain old witches who always came into the kitchen to gossip when Helga was working there. As a result, Helga was always up-to-date on everything and everyone in Witchland. 'How's this Wozo now, Mama?' Mayo asked her mother. 'He was such a meanie in school!' 'He's changed a lot, dear,' Helga replied. 'He's grown up to be quite a gentlewizard. He's not very good at magic, but he is a smart fellow because he realised what he was good at and did just that. He has a business of making cauldrons, which is doing really well. And what a handsome young wizard he has become! He's a little bit of a flirt, though. But then, which wizard of his age isn't?'

That night, Mayo sat at her bedroom window, thinking about Wozo. She didn't know what to make of this wizard. Then, suddenly, out of the deep, black night, Wozo came flying towards her. At first, Mayo thought that she must be dreaming. But she quickly came to her senses when Wozo knocked on the glass pane of the window. Mayo opened the window. Wozo didn't come in but just kept sitting on his broomstick, which now hovered in front of Mayo's window. 'I have come to say sorry, Mayo,' he said, coming straight to the point. 'I know why you reacted the way you did today. You remembered the times in school. I hate those times too, Mayo – I wish I could take them back. I am not proud of the wizard I was back then. And do you know why I troubled you so much? I ... I just needed someone to pick on. I have always been really bad at magic. I always used to fail in all the potion and spell tests. And I used to be teased mercilessly about it at my first school. Everyone said that I was not fit to be a wizard. The teasing became unbearable and that's why my parents had to put me in another school. There I saw that there already was a witch who was the target of the class. I thought that if I joined in teasing her, nobody would notice my shortcomings. But ... but I know this is no excuse, Mayo. What I did was wrong and you have every reason to hate me. But ... but I have changed now, Mayo, and if you give me a chance I'll prove that to you. I'll show you that I can be a good friend too.' Wozo's voice was trembling now, but there was sincerity in it. 'Just think about it Mayo', he said and then sped off on his broomstick.

This sweet speech had begun to melt Mayo's heart. The last bit of it was just about to melt when Tami, who had just come back home for a visit, entered the room. She'd come just in time to see Wozo flying away and now she was curious to know what Wozo had wanted here. Mayo quickly filled her in on the day's happenings. As Tami listened, her eyes bored into Mayo's, as if searching them for something. 'He wants me to be his friend, Tami', Mayo said, her eyes shining. 'He really seems to be a good wizard now.' Tami shook her head disapprovingly. 'I doubt if any witch can be friends with him, for that wizard is a total flirt! He keeps trying to woo all the young witches. Scoot and his bunny friends have told me how they see him every morning in the meadow, plucking daisies for a different witch each time.' 'Oh, don't worry, I'll just be his friend,' Mayo assured her sister.

But such matters cannot be planned or decided. Mayo did start out by being a good friend to Wozo, but she soon fell in love with him. He was such a charming young wizard that any witch would have done the same! Except for his flirting, he really was flawless. He had a kind heart and always reached out to help those in need. He was very dedicated to his work, had a great sense of humour and most importantly, as promised, he was a good friend to Mayo – always there for her, supporting her and cheering her up whenever she remembered the 'itch' incident. But his flirting was incurable! Every evening, when he came down to the café, he would have a new crush to tell Mayo about. And Mayo would laugh it off, knowing that it was never serious. Poor Mayo couldn't muster the courage to tell Wozo how she felt about him. He always treated her just like a good friend – laughing and chatting with her, telling her all his secrets. So Mayo didn't say anything either, but she kept thinking what she could to make him fall in love with her.

One evening, Wozo declared that he was in love with Rizi, one of the most beautiful and clever witches of Witchland. Mayo brushed it aside as just one more of Wozo's crushes. But this crush didn't seem to go away. Days and months passed by with Wozo singing Rizi's praises. He stopped looking at the other witches and kept dreaming about this witch. And then, one fine day, he came down to the café to tell Mayo that he was going to propose to Rizi that night. 'But I don't know what I am going to say or do,' he said nervously. 'Rizi has never paid much attention to me till now.' Mayo listened with a mixture of shock and fear. She felt that her dear Wozo was slipping away from her forever. She had to do something quickly to stop him. She just stood in front of Wozo, lost in thought. 'Hey, Mayo, where are you?' Wozo asked, waving a hand in front of her eyes. 'I'll go to Rizi tonight, but for now I am really hungry. Can you please get me something?'

Mayo suddenly smiled. Now is my chance, she thought, and ran quickly into the house. Wozo, who had seen that smile, wondered what it could have meant. He knew that Mayo loved him – he'd known all along. You could see it in her eyes. But what could he do? He loved her dearly too, but as a friend. Now he sat at the table, trying to figure out why Mayo had smiled like that. He saw Mayo coming out now. She was carrying a bowl. Wozo craned his neck to see what was inside. And then he saw it. It was a light green liquid that was gently bubbling inside the bowl. 'Oh no! Not a love potion!' Wozo exclaimed to himself. 'Why did you have to do that, Mayo? You know I am in love with someone else.' And then, a brilliant idea came to him. 'I'm such a lucky wizard!' He whistled. 'Here I am, in love with a witch and not knowing how to woo her. And then a love potion just falls into my hands. I'm so bad at magic that I would have never been able to make it myself. But there's nothing to stop me now!' He grabbed the bowl from Mayo, said that he was sorry but he would have to take it along and drink it on the way to work as he was getting really late and sped off. Once he was out of the café, he pulled out a glass bottle from his cloak and poured the contents of the bowl into it.

He flew down to Rizi's house that night. He was wearing his best black cloak and had neatly combed his curly black hair. He was carrying the glass bottle in one hand and a bunch of daisies in the other. 'Hello, beautiful witch,' he greeted Rizi, who was sitting outside the house, brushing her black cat. 'Oh my, if it isn't the most handsome wizard who's come to visit!' Rizi said in a faintly mocking tone. 'Here, I've brought you some daisies,' Wozo said. 'And ... and ... some green apple juice,' saying this, he handed over the bottle to her. Rizi looked at it for a moment and smiled. Then, without a word, she lifted it to her lips and drank all its contents. Wozo looked at her expectantly. But before anyone of them could say or do anything, Rizi's mother came out. She was an ugly, old, hunchbacked hag who was always in a bad temper. When she saw Wozo, she flew into a crazy rage. 'What are you doing here?' she shrieked in a piercing voice. 'How dare you come to woo my daughter like this?' she screamed, stamping on the daisies. 'I'll teach you a lesson!' 'Do you want me to

cast a spell on him and make him disappear, Mama?' Rizi asked, standing up.

Wozo stared at her in disbelief. How could she say that about him? Hadn't the love potion worked? 'There's no need to waste any magic on a useless wizard like him,' the old witch spat out. 'My broomstick is good enough for him.' And with that, she fetched her broomstick from inside the house and started beating Wozo with it. Poor Wozo, who just couldn't grasp what had happened, stood stunned, unable to defend himself against the blows that rained on him.

He went to Mayo later that night, covered with bruises and seeking sympathy. Mayo applied medicine to his wounds as he told her what had happened. 'I still don't understand why the love potion didn't work,' he muttered. 'What love potion?' asked Mayo. Wozo bit his tongue, wishing he hadn't spoken out loud. 'Uh ... umm ... the love potion which you gave me, Mayo. I ... I know you ... I am sorry, but ...'

'I didn't give you any love potion,' Mayo said, surprised. 'What?' cried Wozo. 'Then ... then what was that green thing you gave me?' 'That was spinach soup, you silly!' Mayo laughed. So that's why Rizi had drunk it instantly. Wozo understood it now. The clever witch must have known instantly that it was no love potion. The truth was that Mayo could make the most delicious spinach soup. She made it even better than her mother. Helga had told her once that a way to a wizard's heart is through his stomach. So she'd been trying to make Wozo fall in love with her by feeding him her special soup. But of course, she didn't say that to him. An awkward silence hung in the room. And Wozo and Mayo never spoke of this incident later.

Wozo was a changed wizard after that night. He understood how it was to have his heart broken. So he stopped chasing witches and promising them the moon. And now that he wasn't busy flirting, he got the time to understand the true worth of his dear friend, who had always been there for him. He started spending more time with her and it wasn't long before he too fell in love with her. And it wasn't a silly crush this time. It was true love.

One evening, Mayo and Wozo were sitting in the café garden. They were just sitting there, enjoying each other's company and the gentle breeze that was blowing. Wozo was munching on some potato chips. 'You know, these finger chips are my favourite food,' he said suddenly, breaking the silence. 'Mine too.'

Mayo smiled. 'They are nice, crispy and salty.' 'True, but that's not why I like them so much.' Wozo was grinning now. 'Then why do you like them?' Mayo asked curiously. 'Because they always come with mayonnaise!' said Wozo and winked at her. Mayo felt extremely shy all of a sudden. A faint pink blush danced on her cheeks. She felt like running away. 'I ... I have to go inside,' she said. 'I have to bring you your dinner. I have prepared a three-course dinner for you tonight.' And with that, she rushed inside. She soon returned, carrying a bowl of steaming spinach soup. 'Is this a love potion, Miss Mayo?' Wozo asked innocently, but his blue eyes sparkled with mischief. 'You clearly don't know much about magic, Mr Wozo,' Mayo said. 'You cannot give a love potion to someone who is already in love with you. That would make him not love you anymore. And I for sure don't want that!' And they both burst out laughing.

Wozo and Mayo got married later that year. A year after that, Mayo gave birth to a beautiful baby wizard. And the couple named him after their favourite food – Chip!